All Hands on Deck!

Raggedy Rocks

The Roaring Reef

Wicked Whirlpool

Mud Swamps

Spidery Jungle

Treasure Bay

Timber Bay

Parrot Park

Driftwood Dock

Skullabones Town

SKULLABONES ISLAND

The Dump

Vulture Gorge

Dead Man's Cave

Coconut Pit

Deadly Creek

Quicksand Pit

Stinkpot Town

Mosquito Bay

STINKPOT ISLAND

N
W E
S

For Isabel Freya – **RD**

For Mum and Dad – **SH**

LADYBIRD BOOKS

UK | USA | Canada | Ireland | Australia
India | New Zealand | South Africa

Ladybird Books is part of the Penguin Random House group of companies
whose addresses can be found at global.penguinrandomhouse.com.

ladybird.com

Penguin
Random House
UK

First published 2015
001

Ladybird and the Ladybird logo are registered trademarks owned by Ladybird Books Ltd

The moral right of the author and illustrator has been asserted

Printed in China

A CIP catalogue record for this book is available from the British Library

ISBN: 978-0-723-29628-7

Skullabnes Island

All Hands on Deck!

Richard Dungworth ★ Sharon Harmer

The **pirate ship** bobbed gently
as the snow began to fall.
Her captain, on the poop deck,
gave a cheery pirate call…

"ALL HANDS ON DECK,
me hearties!"

"But Captain, it's too cold outside!
We'll **freeze** in all this snow!
A pirate likes the weather **warm**.
We're staying down below!"

"Too cold?" The captain shook his head.
"What nonsense! Winter's **great!**
An icy deck is **splendid** fun.
Come out, you swabs – and **skate!**"

Peeking through the deck-hatch,

Lil thought skating might be nice.

And soon **two** happy pirates

twirled and glided on the ice.

The **pirate ship** bobbed gently
as more snowflakes softly fell.
Her captain, by the mainmast,
gave a cheery pirate yell...

"ALL HANDS ON DECK,
me hearties!"

"But Captain, it's too cold outside!
We'll **freeze** in all this snow!

Our timbers won't stop shivering.

We're staying down below!"

"Too cold?" The captain rolled an eye.
"What twaddle! Snow is **grand!**
Why, **nothing** beats a snowman.
Come on, you lot – lend a hand…"

Peeping through the deck-hatch,

Sam was keen to play his part.

And soon **three** happy pirates

built a snowy work of art.

The **pirate ship** bobbed gently
as the drifts rose all about.
Her captain, on the foredeck,
gave a cheery pirate shout…

"ALL HANDS ON DECK,
me hearties!"

"But Captain, it's too cold outside!
We'll **freeze** in all this snow!
It's cosy in our cabin bunks.
We're staying down below!"

"Too cold?" The captain gave a snort.
"What rubbish! Snow is **fun!**
It's **great** for making angel shapes –
I'll show you how it's done…"

Peering through the deck-hatch,

Tom was itching for a go.

And soon **four** happy pirates

laughed and wriggled in the snow.

The **pirate ship** bobbed gently
underneath the snow-filled sky.
Her captain, at the port side,
gave a cheery pirate cry…

"ALL HANDS ON DECK,
me hearties!"

"But Captain, it's too cold outside!
I'll **freeze** in all this snow!
I'll catch a chill – I **know** I will.
I'm staying down below!"

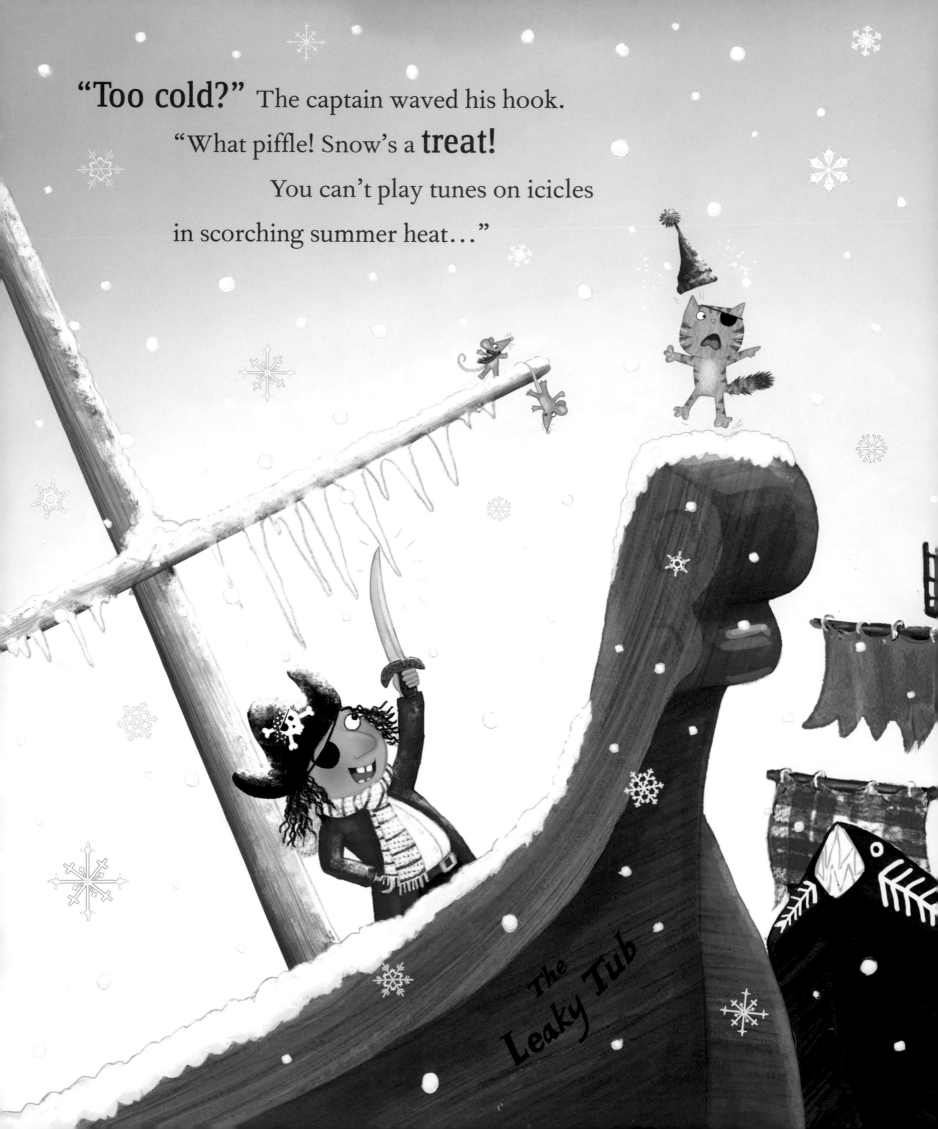

"Too cold?" The captain waved his hook.
"What piffle! Snow's a **treat!**
You can't play tunes on icicles
in scorching summer heat…"

The
Leaky Tub

Watching through the deck-hatch,

Bill felt silly missing out.

And soon **five** happy pirates

sang a song and jigged about.

The **pirate ship** bobbed gently
as the winter light grew dim.
Her captain, on the starboard,
gave a bellow, looking grim.

"STINKYFISH GANG AHOY,
me hearties!"

"But Captain, it's too cold to fight!

What are we going to do?

The cannon are all frozen

and our cutlasses are, too!"

"Don't panic!" cried the captain.

"Hold your nerve, like pirates should!

Our cannonballs are useless,

but here's something **just** as good…"

"Snowballs!" cried the shipmates
as their captain threw the first.
"Of course! Let's pelt the rotters!
Come on, Stinkies – do your worst!"

And so a snowball battle raged
between the pirate foes,
till all were white from head to toe
and pirate fingers froze.

And then – at last – the enemy
turned tail, and sailed away.
And five proud pirates whooped with joy,
"We won! **Ha-haaaar!** Hooray!"

The **pirate ship** bobbed gently
as the snowfall hid the sun.
On deck, five pirate shipmates sang
of battles bravely won.

The snow fell on, and still they sang
of doings brave and bold,
until, at last, their captain cried,
"Let's go below…

…I'm cold!"

Raggedy Rocks

The Roaring Reef

Wicked Whirlpool

Mud Swamps

Spidery Jungle

Treasure Bay

Timber Bay

Parrot Park

Driftwood Dock

Skullabones Town

SKULLABONES
ISLAND